MY BOOK OF WORDS

by Rebecca Heller • illustrated by Robbie Stillerman

A GOLDEN BOOK • NEW YORK

Western Publishing Company, Inc., Racine, Wisconsin 53404

Text copyright © 1982 by Western Publishing Company, Inc. Illustrations © 1982 by Robbie Stillerman. All rights reserved. Printed in the U.S.A. No part of this book may be reproduced or copied in any form without written permission from the publisher. GOLDEN®, GOLDEN & DESIGN®, A FIRST LITTLE GOLDEN BOOK®, and A GOLDEN BOOK® are trademarks of Western Publishing Company, Inc. Library of Congress Catalog Card Number: 81-86491 ISBN 0-307-10131-2/ISBN 0-307-68131-9 (lib. bdg.)   MCMXCIII

cup

bowl

spoon

bib

clock

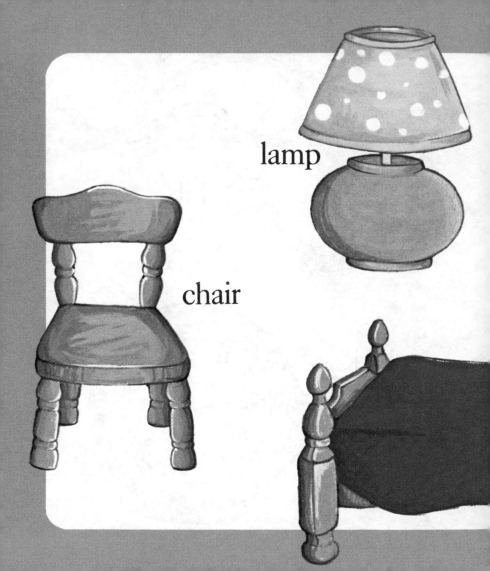

lamp

chair

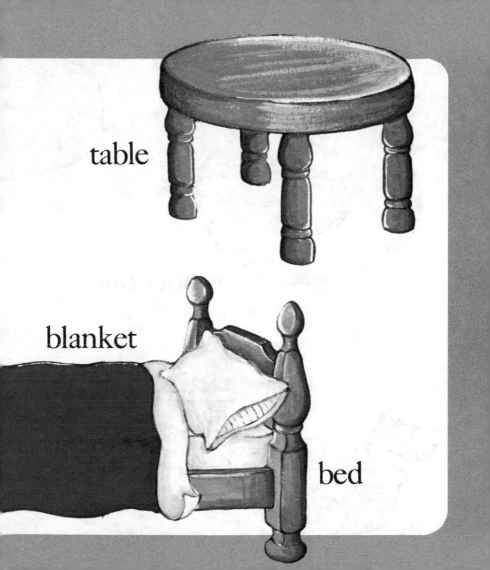

table

blanket

bed

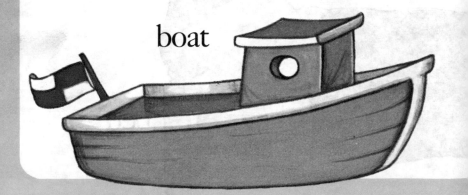

rubber duck

boat

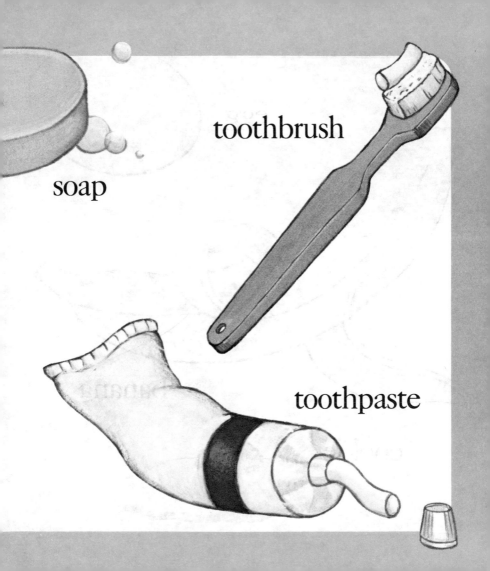

soap

toothbrush

toothpaste

egg

banana

cookie

apple

juice

bread

dress

pants

shoes

coat

boots

sweater

doll

blocks

ball

book

drum

teddy bear

truck

rocking horse

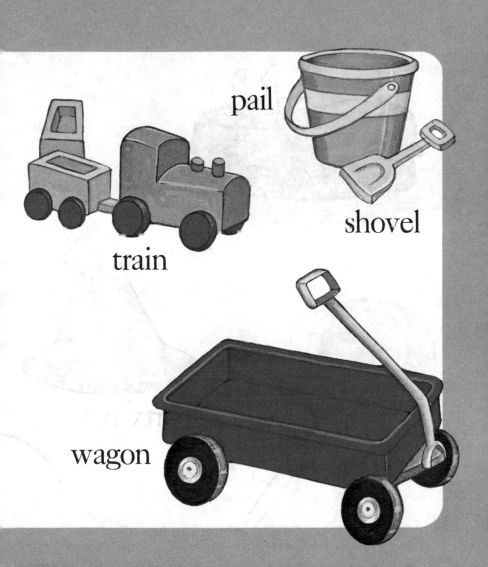

pail

shovel

train

wagon

cake

party hat

lollipop

horn

ice cream

balloon

cat

dog

rabbit

mouse

butterfly

bird

flower

frog

cloud

sun

moon

cloud

tree

house